WHAT'S THE WORD?

By

Lawrence Gordon

A T & P Publishing Book/Published by arrangement with the author.

Printing History
First Printing: April 2016
Copyright 2016 by Lawrence Gordon
Cover Design and production :

For information on booking and bulk orders contact:

ISBN:

Printed in the United States

TABLE OF CONTENTS

PAGE

TABLE OF CONTENTS (cont'd)

PAGE

TABLE OF CONTENTS (cont'd)

DEDICATION

I dedicate this book to my grandmother, Hattie Lee Henderson, and to my uncle, James Henderson, and also to my grandfather, Thomas Henderson; and then to his daughter, my Mom, Bobbie Ann Gordon. I love you Mom. You have been there through everything and you are still standing strong. It's because you are strong that I am strong also—no matter what.

If it weren't for Grandma and Granddad, and Uncle James, no one that I mention would even exist or I may never have known them. I understand that we all have to leave this world one day; so I wanted to put my words on paper. I love you and we are all blessed in our way.

We came from the mud and we're still here, doing well; and we are still improving our lives.

We've shed too many tears, and suffered too much heartache to stop now. I don't have an uncle anymore, but I do have nieces and nephews who look up to me. I realize, too, that much of our family never knew that we had such a hard childhood. It was my duty and I had to let our younger generation of family know that no matter what, our family legacy must continue, it must live on. I want my friends and family to know that they can dream and reach for the stars. There is nothing and no one to stop them.

It's a wonderful feeling to think that Grandma Hattie and Uncle James are looking down on us smiling from Heaven knowing that our job isn't done yet, but also proud and happy that we have made progress.

I just couldn't let my family's name go in vain. So, as I put my words on paper, I hope and pray that I motivate everyone to believe in themselves and believe in God, that He is able to move mountains and set major goals. To my family and friends, I love you. I am still learning and striving myself. Remember the sky is the limit.

These words are true and from my very heart and soul to you all.

'Low'

ACKNOWLEDGEMENTS

My heart is so full of love for many people that to try to acknowledge them individually would take many more pages. So, I want to say that these people listed below are people who were part of my life and helped to shape my character and they also influenced my dream of this book.

I love you all.

Henderson Family, Gordon Family, McCoy Family, Sam Family, Perry Family, Moore Family, Radway Family, Carter Family, Thomas Family, Cody Family, Haley Family, Ming Family, Garner Family, Shorter Family, Hill Family, Gaskins Family, Bullock Family, Johnson Family, Downs Family, Talbert Family, Luckette Family, Hillard/Buster/Perry, Desean

LAWRENCE GORDON

Gordon, Freddie Thomas, Tammy Sams, Stanley Downs, Maurice Downs, Hattie Lee Henderson, James Henderson, James Hayley, Taron Baugh, Reca Daniels, Timothy Brown, Rhonda Stewart, Mrs. Riley, Kareem, Hattie Talbert, Richard/Poon/Allan, Mr. Little, Robert/Poke/Jordan, DBF Mikey, Martha Parker, Gucci, Dorothy Rush, Tony Haley, Mark & Darryl Goings, Ant Ant, Tracey Sharon Clark, White Boy George, Cindy Gaskins, Ernestine Porties, Regina Denise Scott, Lucille Wardlaw, Bigg Mann, DBF George, Uncle Abraham, Talley Family

INTRODUCTION

This is a true story and we are real people.

*****

There was much thought put into this book, as I had to consider that I was going to "spill the beans" about me and my beloved family and friends. I'll tell of a few hurdles we had to jump and of great strides we all made. But even more than that, I wondered if what I wrote about in this book would help or hurt our family.

I have put many hours of prayer into asking God to guide me and praise His Name; He answered and delivered this book into my hands.

*****

Gray Street, where we lived, was like a coliseum. Gladiators were trained for the sport of fighting. They received the skills they needed to fight and survive. In the same way, our neighborhood was a lot like that.

We could learn behaviors as praiseworthy as good manners or deplorable behaviors like 'street pimpin.' This was the 'university of street living' or 'streets r us'. If someone failed a class in this "higher learning institution," it could lead to prison or even death. In this same environment I acquired survival skills. Oddly, I learned to believe in a higher power and I learned to love.

The same neighborhood was a drug infested area. I want you to know that there is nothing sweet or good about selling drugs, period. Many of those that I love, family and friends already understand that statement. However, for those people reading this book, please pay attention to this one concept I want to get across to you: Regardless of your environment and no matter where you reside, good seeds can be planted and also bad seeds can be planted. Obstacles can be overcome and struggles can lead to success. This is so no matter where you are in this world.

It is my sincere hope that after reading this book you are inspired and motivated to reach for your own dream, no matter the circumstances. I desire that this story teaches you not to point a finger at someone or something else, but to always look at yourself first, then make the changes you need to make to achieve your goals.

****

So — WHAT'S THE WORD?

The word is that I want to thank God first and foremost for all He has done.

WHAT'S THE WORD?

This is a work of non-fiction. The events penned herein reflect real life situations; great times and terrible times; which my family, my friends, and I endured.

This work will reflect the spiritual aspects of my family. I was born and raised in our family church. The name of the church was God's Universal House of Prayer and my Uncle, James Henderson was the Pastor until he passed away. Since my Uncle never married or had any children, his mother, who was also my grandmother, Hattie Lee Henderson was the church's first lady. Grandma Hattie was always there for everyone, no matter what.

WHAT'S THE WORD?

Because of some of the events I revealed in this book, the decision was made to change some of the names of the persons mentioned.

WHAT'S THE WORD?

Because this story is about our family it will focus on greatness and also look back on some of the best of times and the worst of times. I will tell of our trials and how we overcame them. I wrote it as my heart gave it to me and not in any specific date order.

Violence, education, music, professions, and businesses will be mentioned in these pages. Good things and ugly things will also be revealed to everyone reading this piece so as to let everyone in the world understand that the environment and circumstances that surround you don't have to swallow you up. You can still be successful in this life. Success has many faces: Health, knowledge, teaching, and parenting. Success can be simply blessing others.

****

I love my family. I know that families have arguments, fights and even death; but at the end of the day, it doesn't matter how you slice it, cook it or cut it—they are still your family, your blood.

With that thought I want to say once more that this is my story, not a series or a fraudulent TV show with actors. There are some in my family who didn't believe in this book. They didn't share the vision. No matter, those members are mentioned, too.

I thank God again for touching my heart to write this epic story. I give Him all the glory.

CHAPTER ONE: THE FOUNDATION

On April 6, 1988, I arrived at my Grandma Hattie's house to help her move from Gray Street. I was 12 years old then; and like most dummies my age, I thought I knew it all. My mom, Bobbie Gordon, told me to stay in the house and wait until she got back home and she would take me over my grandma's house herself. She was away visiting one of her best friends Rina or Miss Flo. I really didn't care. So I caught the bus and then walked from East Seymour Street to Gray Street, where some of my family members lived and one of my good friends, James Hayley lived.

My two older brothers, Michael Henderson and D.K., along with three older sisters; a niece, Diane and two little nephews, Antonio and Tony, all lived there on Gray Street. Tony and Antonio's mom was my sister, Deborah Henderson. My brother D.K. was my niece Diane's dad. D.K. was also my mom's firstborn and was attending Adrian College at that time; studying and getting degrees in Math and actually majoring in Accounting.

Though D.K. was educated, he was probably the dumbest one in our family. He walked with his pride and chin up, but looked down on others who were not educated. That's dumb.

Additionally, most of the family didn't respect him, not because of his education, but because of how he treated our grandmother. Even though I was his brother, I, too, stayed away from him. It really is a true saying: "The Devil is a liar".

CHAPTER TWO: SHALL BE KNOWN AS 'THE GAME'

I have one sister, Carla Thomas who is older than my sister Deborah, Tony and Antonio's mom. Out of the eight children that my mom had, Carla was very complicated. She got married some years before and she tended to stay to herself. On Sundays she was a church woman; but the rest of the week well, she was a nurse or a counselor. Actually it really didn't matter because no one listened to her or gave a damn about what she was talking about most of the time. Our house was a two family flat like all the homes on Gray St. And there were six to seven people living downstairs in the house.

In the upstairs flat lived my Aunt Carleine's daughter, Rosalind Downs and her four children and Aunt Carleine's grandchildren. That meant that there were young adults and their children living upstairs; they were around the same age as me or slightly older.

My dear mom's name is Bobbie Gordon. She has three sisters, Jonny, Carleine, and Louise. She also had one brother, my one and only uncle, James Henderson.

My mom and her sisters each had their own families, but like a lot of families, they would often visit their own mother and their brother's home.

I lived with my mom on Seymour Street. My early life is important to me and I share it now because I love my family dearly. My third older sister Robin Gordon, and two younger sisters, Latonja and Danyell Gordon all lived with my mom. My little sister Latonja and I have the same father. However, our last name Gordon is from my sister Robin's father

In our neighborhood the majority of the homes were two family flats. At that time there weren't many people with cell phones. The high tech device then was a beeper. There certainly weren't many computers, either. Typically, in our homes there was a big T.V. with a smaller T.V. sitting on top of the big one.

Sadly, guns were still available; but people then were not preying on one another to kill each other. We all knew the people who had the guns, too—policemen and drug dealers.

As I mentioned, on that particular weekend, I was helping my Grandma Hattie to move from Gray Street. It was around five or six in the evening and I had been walking around for a while, because I got lost going over there.

When I got to her house I was greeted by my Grandma yelling, "Why you leave your mother's house?"

I told her, "To help you move, Grandma."

"Oh, okay. Well get them boxes and put them in the front for in the morning, (we are moving off Gray Street in the morning) grandson."

I remember thinking when Grandma said that, I was safe from being disciplined by my mom.

All that back and forth with my mom about me leaving was over. My Grandma Hattie had nipped that in the bud for me quickly.

So, on this day of packing up Grandma Hattie's house getting her ready to move out the next day, I got to having fun outside with my Brother Michael, my Sister Deborah and some of my cousins and nephews. In my neighborhood and in my family we played outside until the street lights came on. When the street lights came on that meant that it was time to come in the house, close the door, and don't ask or think about going outside again that night. When those street lights came on you didn't say, "Okay, just a minute" or "I'm coming". It was immediately in the house and shut the door. That was about nine p.m.

Uncle James and the rest of us were all in this house cluttered with boxes to be moved the next day. We were still packing up as fast as we could, too because the next night was Saturday WWF Wrestling – The Main Event. My Uncle James was a big wrestling and boxing fan and so were my nephews and me. We were so excited because we wanted to see some of our favorite wrestlers, like Hulk Hogan and the Ultimate Warrior. My Uncle James was also excited about the move. We spent our time talking about the move and wrestling.

JAMES HENDERSON PATRIARCH OF OUR FAMILY AND A REAL MAN

My Uncle James Henderson was the patriarch of our family. He was the only son that my grandmother had. He was a truly good man. Just like my grandma, Uncle James loved his family, his siblings and his nieces and nephews. He was the pastor of our family church, and he preached God's word.

Uncle James loved wrestling. He'd sit around along with the rest of us and watch and enjoy wrestling events on T.V. He was also an avid jogger. Uncle James would jog from our home on Gray Street to Belle Isle and back. He did this about three times a week!

It is interesting too, that Uncle James never married and I can't say that I ever even saw him with a woman friend. He never used bad language either. And though he didn't have a girlfriend or wife, he was all man, and I mean all man. I believe that he saw his family and dedicated his life to helping all of us and setting the correct example not just for his nephews, but also for his nieces. There was no one like Uncle James. He showed us the right way to go, how to live and behave. If we didn't do it, the fault was ours not his. He was a true man of God.

CHAPTER THREE:
THE "WHITE GIRL'S" WICKED WAYS

We were having a great time sprawled out in Uncle James' and Grandma's house that night having a lot of fun talking about moving to the new house and different wrestling matches. About 25 minutes after the house settled down and got quiet as we all went to bed or were getting ready for bed I was sitting around waiting patiently for my Uncle James to finish in the bathroom so I could wash up, relax and get ready for bed. Suddenly all I could hear was the loud pops of a barrage of bullets being fired on the outside of our house.

The bullet shots were on the side of the house where my Grandma, my two young nephews, who were five and two at the time, and my Uncle were. Gun fire! I was half asleep when it happened so when I opened my eyes all I could see was dust and wood flying around in the air everywhere! Gun fire!

I had been dreaming about wrestling and a new house; so you can imagine that I was still in a daze from what was happening. I could hear screams! I snapped out of that illusion to see bullets hitting my Uncle James in his neck area— his throat!

I couldn't believe, what I was witnessing at that very moment. So, I tried to get up out the chair as I screamed out, "Uncle". I was going to try to rush over to him and help him, but suddenly a bullet hit me in the shoulder. I never would have thought that this misfortune would have happened to my uncle. I dropped like a fly out of air.

Even though I was wounded, I could still hear and see everything going on around me. My uncle choking on blood, gun fire still erupting, I'm down under the table from the blast force of the bullet penetrating my flesh. I remember that I was thinking, "I can't believe this is even happening at my family's house! At a Pastor's house! At my grandmother's house! No! What the hell?!"

Right about then I turn and see my little nephew Antonio come out of the room where my grandma was.

I started yelling at him, "Get outta here little boy!"

He didn't know what to do or think. He was a baby at the time.

"Get outta here!" I screamed at him.

It was then that I saw my cousin, Maurice Downs. He had come downstairs from upstairs. He was trying to help my Uncle James. Maurice didn't know at that time that I was hit, also. He and my uncle were saying something. I couldn't hear clearly what they were saying at first. But the one thing that I did hear my uncle say clearly to Maurice was: "Keep the family together." Now I did hear my uncle say that.

Within approximately 20-25 minutes I see ambulances and police cars on our street. I was put on a stretcher. My uncle was nowhere within my sight. I was driven by ambulance to the emergency room.

I saw the doctor when I came to early Saturday morning, and I immediately asked him about my uncle. Deep down inside I really already knew he was dead. But I asked anyway.

The doctor said, "Bad news, son. He didn't make it."

After speaking with the doctor, I just laid there in disgust and disbelief at what had just took place in front of my very own eyes! I was just shaking my head and crying terribly. I was sore, staring up at the ceiling thinking that this is a dream, no a nightmare. But it wasn't. It was real. And I had the scar from a bullet to remind me every day that it wasn't a dream.

Chapter Four

NELIGENCE ROAMS DEEP WITHIN

On the next day, April 7th, my family and friends helped my Grandma move away from Gray Street. They could clearly see the bullets from the gun fire we had endured the night before.

Needless to say, everyone was still in shock at my uncle's senseless and violent death. I was still in the hospital getting patched up. Frustrated, I knew that soon I would be on my way to the new house. I was emotionless and still tearing up from the memories of that night. Only God and my uncle could feel my pain. I was an innocent bystander. Fuck!

I had just arrived at the new house from the hospital. My family members were all over the place crying in disbelief about my uncle and making funeral arrangements for 'Unc.' While this is happening I'm lying there and everyone, my mom, sisters, brothers, aunts, cousins and nephews are wearing very sad faces crying again in disbelief and concern for me. I'm blessed, though. Little did they know, it didn't hurt. I just felt a hot iron pressed against my skin for a few short seconds.

I was, however, really out done with this terrible change of events. My uncle, the backbone of our family had just gotten bullet riddled to death.

Just like that. It changed my mind and my thoughts on life burying my loved one. I learn at that young age that when God says, "You know what? I want you in My Kingdom, there is nothing you can do about it. How you go, don't matter. How you're living—You outta here. Period. I faced that reality early in my life. And I'm still dealing with that.

At the funeral and burial of my beloved Uncle, I was very confused and I asked my family questions like, "What the fuck?! How did some bull shit like this even happen?!"

My cousin, Kevin Downs, who lived upstairs from my uncle, began telling his story. When the story was told the argument that led to the shootout was about a girl, money (less than $75.00) and drugs—bottom line.

My cousin Kevin and his so called buddies got into an argument with some other street guys earlier that day. My family and I didn't know anything about it. We were totally in the dark about that argument and that made us sitting ducks.

Those street guys had their gun off 'cock mode' and were ready for whatever. They were firing at my cousin and his friends. Kevin and his friends started running toward our house. Those street guys were aiming at them and ready to kill whoever was in the way. Pulling their triggers over and over again—Yes. These guys weren't playing any games. They were firing bullets, bullets that killed my uncle and wounded me in my shoulder. It's true. These dudes didn't care what the fuck or who the fuck they killed. Sadly, there was no telling who my cousin and his friends had murdered at the same time, themselves.

Months went by after the shooting and my body healed; but I was destroyed on the inside. I started back to school. I went to Columbus Middle School. It was there that I found basketball. I loved it, too. My friends and I played hoops every day.

CHAPTER FIVE

AM I MY BROTHER'S KEEPER?

Like I was saying, my friends and I had a love for basketball and we played it all the time. Playing basketball sort of helped me during the grieving process over my uncle. It filled in a lot of 'space' for me.

It was while the family was trying to heal emotionally that we discovered my older brother, D.K's devious ways. After my uncle passed,

D.K. wanted to be the Boss, the King, and he felt he was superior to everyone else. He was consumed with the desire for power and the desire for money.

He even took advantage of my Grandma Hattie, convincing her that since my uncle was gone, she should put his name on the deed to the new house on Old Town street, where she had moved to. He gave her the 'logical' argument that it was necessary since at the time; he was the only one with a job.

My grandma, thinking he was right and would do right, did as he asked. She had no idea that he would take the house from her and not just the house, he took all the furniture, as well. He took the new house that was in Old Town that my uncle paid for. He took it from his own grandmother. What a dick move! WACK D.K. WACK!

It was such a heinous act that there were vicious arguments between him and other family members. It even got violent a few times at that house on Old Town. He got into it with my other brother, Michael. D.K. knew how to manipulate everyone with his college and dictionary vocabulary.

I just couldn't get to how my grandma let this fool do that to her. Years have gone by and I still go back and forth with it.

After that terrible incident, some months went by and one day my grandma said, "Hey I found us a house."

We all asked her what she meant.

She said, "Let him have it."

I asked her if she was serious and she was. I didn't have any money to make any demands on the situation or to have an opinion about it. Wow.

CHAPTER SIX

NEW BEGINNING—WAYBURN STREET

On Wayburn street our family began a fresh and new start. We had an integrated neighborhood with black and white people. The neighbors were cool. We also had a basketball rim in the backyard. YES! It was during this time in my growing up that Jukebox was hot and we watched videos all day.

Back on Gray Street my friends were 'grindin' and hustling. Doing whatever it took to get a dollar, to get that money. While they were 'grinding' I was going to Columbus Middle School and I graduated from Columbus after completing the 8th Grade. That was cool, too.

I started Denby High School in my freshman year. Because I saw a lot of my middle school classmates in Denby, I wasn't so nervous going to a much larger school. But the twelfth grade boys looked like grown men, at first.

One day in my freshman year, while going to class I saw a notice for basketball tryouts at the school — The Tars Basketball Team. I also saw the basketball coach. His name was Coach Rubinstein Washington. He was a short man but he talked very big.

The basketball stars, at the time, was Senior Guard Emmanuel Bibbs and Senior Guard Andre Williams. And both of them were balling, too.

My friends and I tried out for the team and made it. That's when I met new friends other than those I had on Gray Street and those in middle school. Their names were Mike J, Ken, Todd, Wally, Antonio, Sean, and Kib. I met many others, but these guys are just a few of them. We would usually all meet up at each other's house to play basketball.

While I am with my new friends, my friends from Gray Street were still 'grinding' and running the streets doing whatever to get that dollar. Because my grandma had moved away from Gray Street to Wayburn Street, I was not with my Gray street friend very much.

Even so, there was one friend from Gray Street that I stayed in contact with — James Hayley. James was about two years older than me and he looked like LeBron James. He along with the others was still doing things their own way. The false way.

At Denby, we were getting ready for the Cross Country Team. If a student played basketball for Denby, he could also run track and run cross country. He could also be on the Junior Varsity team. A student who played basketball at Denby always had a team he could be on. Because of that I spent my high school years struggling to get a passing grade in classes, dating and missing my morning classes. We were always at practice, no matter what.

While I struggled through school, my brother, Michael Henderson, became interested in rap music all the time. He had a group called 94 East.

Now, I want it known that my whole family did some type of music: The boys played the drums in church. The girls sang in the choir at church-we all sang in the choir for that fact; and my Mom, Bobbie Gordon played the organ. She still plays the organ to this day.

As expected, when graduation time came around I had to face the fact that a few friends from Denby and I 'bull shitted' all through school, skipping classes, playing ball, and not focusing at all on school and our grades.

What was worse during these high school years is that my little nephews were watching all of this at their young ages. My nephew, Antonio, even fell in love with the rap game. I wound up having to go to summer school and graduated from there. At least I graduated from high school. I continued to do what I wanted, dating and having fun — too much fun because my girlfriend at the time, Denise Gaskin, went on to have a beautiful little baby girl named Tanika Gordon.

So, I thought college would save me.

CHAPTER SEVEN
SOME THINGS NEVER CHANGE

With a baby, I had to man up quickly, "Ferris State University here I come."

My boy Kib from high school and I both filled out applications to Ferris State and we were both accepted.

In the meantime, my Grandma Hattie was getting older and getting sicker because she had asthma and continued to smoke. She smoked Eve

120s. I'll never forget that brand. Along with all of that she continued to deal with my uncle's passing.

I went to visit my boys on Gray Street and I told them that I was on my way to Ferris State. All of them were so happy for me. I really just couldn't believe it. My buddy, James Hayley was super hyped for me and he whispered in my ear, "You do that 'Low'. ('Low' was my nickname). "Yeah, 'Low', you do that. My dude! 'Cause I got some business in Alabama".

He didn't tell what that business was. So, we all hugged and slapped five for hours. Then I went back to Wayburn Street to pack for the winter semester at Ferris State with housing.

I loved it, too; for all the wrong reasons. I had freedom 100 miles away from my grandma and my mom.

I told myself, "Oh yeah I'm outta here. We even got an old friend to take us. Sweet!"

"Oh yeah," Kib said. "We there."

Mike J was already there, too and a few more good friends. Word!

So when we got to Ferris we spent our time partying and bull shitting real heavy. We had room, board, and a meal plan. We even met other guys on campus who were managers. One was a manager in a clothing department and the other was a manager in a restaurant. We were good to go for a year and a half … until grades came out.

"Damn Bro," I said. "Our grades is terrible."

The next semester, Kib said, "We done."

"Fuck", I said thinking of my mom and grandmother.

It was back to reality and back to Detroit, Michigan where Grandma ruled. We knew that we were living totally out of order up here and things got worse. It was so out of order and bad that my daughter's mother let her come and stay with me a whole month. It wasn't like I was really doing anything at school.

My daughter being with me for that amount of time was really cool. While all of this was going on, I had my daughter with me. I knew we were about to get kicked out of school. Our grades were terrible and our funds were gone. After we were kicked out of school, I went back to Wayburn Street in Detroit.

By the time we were kicked out of school and got back home, my brother and his girlfriend Quita were living together. So it was my Grandma Hattie, my sister Deborah, my two nephews and me living on Wayburn Street. And even though my grandma was still trying to smoke those Eve 120s, she was getting around pretty good and she was still going to church. I was back in church a little bit, but then I really had no choice.

My nephew, Antonio was playing drums for the church; and my nieces were singing in the choir. Like I said before that is what my family does – music.

I ran into an old friend from Gray Street. He asked me, "Low what's up my dude? What you doing back so fast? What happened?"

I told him, "Man that school had a rat problem," lying to him. But in my head I was saying that my grades were a disaster.

"Damn, what you gonna do?" he asked, hunching his shoulders up and down like a cat.

"Get a job, I guess. I'm not sure, my dude."

Then suddenly he burst out and said, "You know James Hayley went to prison."

"What the hell?" I shouted. Then asked him why he went to prison.

All he said was that something went down in Alabama.

"Damn," I said. "He did say he had some business to take care of." I didn't know what business he was talking about.

"He got some time, too, Low," my friend said.

I shook my head once again. We finished our conversation and I went back to Wayburn Street.

CHAPTER EIGHT
RUNNING FROM ONE SITUATION TO ANOTHER

I was thinking about James Hayley saying to myself, "Damn. Before I went to Ferris State, he said to me, "Oh, 'Low' it's going down. Go on to school. I was thinking about my baby girl, also. I was thinking about all of that while I was on my way to my Grandma Hattie's house and while I was there.

Then I heard Grandma Hattie say, 'Low', black boy, do you hear me talking to you?"

"Yes," I said.

"Go get me some cigarettes!" she demanded.

Upset with her, I said, "Granny, you already coughing, and you have asthma!"

She looked at me and said, "You want to keep living in my house and eating my food for free …"

I didn't say anything, I just looked at her. I was clueless, at the time.

"…then go get me my Eve 120s," she finished.

I just shook my head. But, while I was getting the money I said, "Grandma, I'm going to get a job real soon and this is gonna be over for you real soon, too. I'm not getting you no more smokes."

While I was making my little speech, Grandma Hattie was rolling her eyes at me.

"Just go get them, 'Low.'"

This continued for some months until winter time. I came in one day and happily told her, "Hey Grandma I found a job at a warehouse, cleaning up."

"Congrats, grandson. When do you start?"

"Next week," I told her.

"Oh, okay. Go to the store for me," she asked.

"Aww Grandma come on," I said.

She looked at me as if to say, "You don't have a check yet."

I just shook my head again.

Then she said to me, "Grandson, this is the last time. I promise."

I said, "Okay Grandma."

So, I began working and making a few bucks. The motto in our home was: "Some money is better than none." I even managed to save some money, too. But while I was working, my granny's health was getting worse and worse and she was on oxygen from having asthma and smoking for so many years.

Day after day I watched her get worse and to add to the stress of my granny's situation, one of my sisters was having a relationship with a 'loser' that she was in love with. It was a back and forth situation.

My sister, Deborah Henderson, was so in love with this no good dirty snake; and she was neglecting our granny and her own sons. My grandma, who didn't care for this guy either, watched this scenario for months along with the rest of us until she had had enough. She told my sister that he couldn't come over to our house anymore. He disrespected my sister all the time, and she allowed it to happen. So, when Grandma Hattie told her he couldn't come over anymore, the two of them moved together. It was a terrible move on my sister's part because she became a prisoner in his house. And she didn't tell us what was going on.

The man was just a coward, acting as if my sister was too busy for her sons, my nephews. We all saw the situation for what it was, but we let it be. We tried to focus on what we were doing and in reality, what we were doing was a little bit of nothing. It was during this time that my one nephew, Antonio developed a passion for hip hop and rap music. He engaged in little 'rap battles' in our neighborhood—Wayburn and Morang area. He even formed a little group called "New Skool." Even though they practiced all the time at the house, and they were looking like stars with big money; in truth, they were broke as hell.

So, I continued to work and my nephews had to watch over our grandma. They both really helped out a lot. My nephews would cook sausages and noodles, the kind of things that a 15 year old and a 12 year old could cook.

Chapter nine
CIRCUMSTANCES MAKE BOYS BECOME MEN

When I took inventory of my life to that point, I was back home from school because I was kicked out for having terrible grades; and I was working in a dead end job that wasn't going nowhere.

I was dating women left and right, 'soiling my loin' because I was using protection for the women I didn't know too well and no protection for the ones I did know. I did that often. As I think about it I had no real answers for why I did that. I was playing Russian Roulette with my penis. And playing the sex game like that with no self-control will eventually catch up with you.

And it caught up with me. I got another woman pregnant and had a son, Lawrence Gordon, Jr. The following year I had another son, Jaylen Gordon. I was recklessly juggling women and I got three children. Wow! What a change in my life. It was a drastic change that was difficult for me. But as for my two sons and my beautiful daughter, I wouldn't change a thing. I love them all; no matter what.

But once again I became involved the whore life, sneaking around and in and out of my grandma's house. I thought she really didn't know about it as I used my room off to the side in the basement. I had my own bathroom, too. My grandma very rarely came down there. But as I look back, Grandma Hattie probably knew all along. She just didn't make a big deal of it. I guess she thought that I was home and if she needed me, I was close by.

Through it all, my Grandma Hattie had a genuine love for her family. Whatever made you happy, she was fine with it; even when I had a few women come by the house unannounced.

The bottom line is that I am alive and I have been blessed after I chose to live that life. There are consequences to everything you do. I was told that it ain't what you do, it's how you do it.

My grandma always taught us to do things decently and in order. And I confess that I wasn't doing things in order. Now I had my kids and my nephews and nieces looking up to me. I had to make a change in my life. My uncle was gone, so I didn't have him. I did have younger kids, the younger generation watching me and we did learn good family morals. I knew that I was nothing like my uncle, but I also knew that I could improve myself. Once you know better, usually you can do better. I wasn't trying to hurt anyone's feelings. I was just living my life. I loved beautiful women.

I learned that I was just young, dumb and full of it; and just being hard headed. I kept bumping my head until I had had enough of bumping it. There was no excuse because my mother, Bobbie Gordon and my Grandma Hattie had taught me to always respect women. I just didn't listen. What's that saying? "A hard head makes a soft bottom." And I am a firm believer that you reap what you sow. I have had my share of miserable experiences with trying to be a player. It was terrible.

GRANDMA HATTIE HENDERSON –
THE ONE AND ONLY!

I loved my Grandma Hattie. In fact, all of her grandchildren loved her. There was no one like her. She loved her family, all of them. Her one desire was for us to stay together, help one another, and succeed. Grandma was the matriarch of our family and she was also the first lady of our family church. She was faithful to God like she was faithful to her children and grandchildren. She loved us and we all knew it.

Whenever we were around her, we had no doubt that she cared dearly for all of us; even when she knew that we weren't right or living as we should have. She never abandoned us because of our behavior. We may have thought that she was ignorant of what we were doing, but not so. She was kind and wise at the same time.

Chapter Ten

TURNING BOYS INTO MEN

Then on one Michigan winter night there was a blizzard. There was snow everywhere. That's just Michigan weather and you get accustomed to it. But this particular night seemed to be the worst night for winter.

We were all home and watching T.V. It was late when all of a sudden my nephew, Antonio started yelling out to me, "Unc', Unc' Grandma not breathing!"

When I heard that I thought to myself, "Shit. What do I do?"

My nephews and I were puzzled at first. Then I said, "Call 911," while I was hollering and screaming and crying, "Grandma, wake up, please."

We put her in my car and raced to the St. John Hospital Emergency Room. The look on our faces was one of disbelief. We had no words to utter, but we did get her to the hospital in time and the doctors were able to save her life that night. We called my mom, my aunts and other family members and they all got there a little later. It was such a scare, a close call. We all felt so helpless.

When the time came that we could go in to see Grandma Hattie, she had tubes everywhere and IVs in her arm. She looked exhausted. All of us teared up to see her that way. Then she began trying to talk to us, but we couldn't understand what she was trying to say. We could tell that it hurt her to try to talk. What she was trying to say was that we are all on borrowed time and to get your business in order, all of us, family and friends. I didn't have a clue at the time what business I had to get in order. But my grandma was saying her last goodbyes to us. She was tired now and not motivated to live anymore for this life.

Grandma stayed in the hospital for a few days. She got her strength back and was able to come home to Wayburn Street. All the family members called and checked on her more often. We would have conversations more often about if she passed away. She was talking better and eating better, which was good.

But my nephews and I were not thinking clearly. We would tell her, "Grandma you feel better. Why are you still talking about God's Kingdom? We already had that big scare, Grandma. That's over now. We just didn't understand.

So, granny didn't say much more. She was looking like someone at Christmastime, happy and full of joy and the spirit. She said to us "Grandsons, I love ya'll. No matter what goes on ya'll stick together and help one another. Work on yourselves so you can better the family."

When she said that, Antonio, Lil Tony and me just started hugging each other. We made a pact that we were going to grind hard on that music, not really realizing how true that statement was.

Some months later, my Grandma Hattie passed away in her sleep. I remember my cousin giving her mouth to mouth over and over and over again; but this time it was the end and we all knew it. The ambulance did come and our neighbors came out, too. Grandma Hattie had passed away.

When my grandma's funeral came around, it was a sad, sad day. The neighborhood came out to pay their respects. We had the funeral and buried her. Once again I was thinking to myself, "What am I going to do? We have already lost greatness; and now the seed. This is a strange feeling."

My nephews and I continued living in the house on Wayburn Street, but it was a mess. We didn't have any money and were broke. I knew that I needed to get some extra money quick. I registered for the Michigan Barber School. They accepted my application and I received a grant to pay for it.

That was a surprise to me after what happened at Ferris State. While I was attending barber school, I found a barber shop to work in on the west side of town in the Joy Road area. The work was slow, but steady and I was glad because I was still a barber student and getting' all the sauce.

My grandma had paid for that house on Wayburn Street where my nephews and I were staying; so all we had to pay was the DTE bill and the water bill. That was good and we managed to do that.   I was working and my nephew was getting' that music poppin'. We were all grinding together.

But we were still disgusted at how we were living. One thing is that the music business is up and down; and if you're not passionate about your music, then it's game over. You've already lost if you're in music for a quick buck and you haven't done your homework, game over. My nephew Antonio, as I said before had made a name for himself. He was known as 'Tone-tone' the Rapper. His label was DBF meaning 'Da billionaire Family.' We weren't rich yet, but we knew that it was going to happen one day. We had done too much grinding, crying and endured too much pain to settle for peanuts. We wanted to be successful and wealthy.

In the midst of all of this we got some great news—James Hayley was back around. He was back home from the big house. We were really focused now and we were hyped because James Hayley, who looked even bigger, was there and we needed him for power because it is really true,

the haters are very real in Detroit.

CHAPTER ELEVEN
THE RAP GAME GLAMORIZES WHAT THE YOUNG CATS WANT 'THE GOOD LIFE"

My nephews and I were working very hard. We even began networking with other CEOs of other groups who were under the same umbrella organization as we were. Our lives were working and making music. Regardless how it looked on the outside, our pockets were screaming 'feed us, feed us.

We were very busy trying to make our dreams come true. But on the inside I was dying because of the grief, pain and heartache I had endured. People looking at us from the outside had no clue how I was feeling. I put on a 'poker face' to the outside world. They were like, "Ya'll ballin'. But to myself I was like, "Okay, we crackin.'"

So, we continued grindin, Tone-Tone was doing beats; and I was doing beats, too. Our other family members were believing in us as we were working and making moves; doing our best living our lives in Detroit, Michigan where only the strong survive. Don't misunderstand, it's rough here, but it is also home.

As I said before James Hayley was there with us all the way. He was a driving force to help us continue to be successful.

But one day, James said, "Hey fellas, I'm getting tired of this. This has been going on for many years."

James was battling cancer all the time he was working with us. But he didn't say anything and we didn't know it. He was still working hard with us all the time. But then he started staying away from us for long periods of time. He was going through different stages and going through with his own family. But we didn't know that, at the time. And he was putting distance between us and him. But he finally broke down and told me.

He came to me one day and said, "Low."

When I saw him, I said, "What man? I haven't seen you in weeks, months, James. You a hater, my dude? You see what we tryin' to do. You wack, Bro? Where you been?"

Right then, before I could say another vulgar word, he said, "I got cancer."

"Why would you just say that for nothing? Who would say they got cancer playing around? Nobody, man. Cancer ain't no joke, that's a serious matter." I waited for him to say it was a joke but he stood there with a straight face. I said, "James…"

He simply said, "'Low,' I'm going to die in 8 to 9 months from now. 'Low,' it's over for me."

I didn't want to accept that. I said, Bro' you are acting real weak right now. We are gonna beat this, Bro'. Look, you're still strong; you look healthy, my dude."

"Lawrence Gordon…" he said using my full name, "…I'm going to die, my dude 8 to 9 months from now. Stop denying what I'm saying, 'Low.'"

It was too much. I was just amazed how a person could say, "I'm going to die," and mean those words.

In the days ahead we would always talk and laugh and have good and friendly conversations. All the while I was thinking to myself, "Oh, he is going to beat this." And I even said it to him, too. He just said, "Okay, 'Low'."

Time continued on and even though James was taking Chemotherapy, he didn't look too different to me. He would be tired after his Chemo treatments and understandably he'd get depressed.

I was back working, cutting hair and doing music grinding, too. One day when I was on my way home, I pulled into a gas station to get some gas. It was still early in the day. When I went into the station, a dude was in there robbing it!

I said, "Fuck that!" Then I turned around to run away and the dude shot his gun in my direction and hit the steel door. The force of the steel door smashed my leg. I thought I had been shot. I couldn't believe it. There was a pain in my leg that I can't describe. I still managed to run to my car and drive off. As I was driving, I looked down at the gas pedal to see how much blood was on the floor, but there wasn't any blood at all. I was wondering, "What the hell?"

I pulled over to check my foot, but I couldn't put any pressure on it. I was cussin' and swearing. I said, "What the shit!" When I tried to get out of the car, my foot felt like I was walking on water. There was no feeling and I couldn't control my foot. It was weak like a noodle. I just didn't know what to think. I did manage to drive myself to the hospital. When I got around to the emergency room entrance, I blew my horn and yelled to the people, "Yo' I can't walk. I need some help."

So they came out and helped me into the hospital. I had told the doctor that I thought my ankle might be sprung.

After examination, the doctor said, "Sir, you have a ruptured Achilles."

Then I said, "Umm 3-4 weeks?"

He said, "No. Try 1 to 2 years."

I yelled, "What?" I just started shaking my head and asked, "What now?"

He said, "cast after cast."

It was then that I just lost it. I screamed out, "Fuck the world. God damn. God, what else are you trying to prove to me?"

So much had happened and now the drama with my foot. I was feeling helpless at this point.

I felt like I was at the mercy of anyone. I was having a real hard time dealing with this. I was so full of what was happening to me at that point. I was so out of it that for a while I forgot about my best friend, who was dealing with cancer.

But soon I calmed down and began the process of getting my foot better. I was fitted with a cast, like the doctor said and I was also on crutches.

While this was going on, my friend, James' body had started to deteriorate badly. I would call him and there was no answer. I really couldn't get around because of the cast and I was still on crutches. I'd call again and still there was no answer. I was determined to see what the hell was going on. So, I called his brother John.

He said, 'Low,' you gotta come see him. There's nothing they can do for him, at this point."

I just held the phone, shaking my head and crying.

CHAPTER TWELVE
TURNING DREAMS INTO REALITY

I found out what hospital James was in. I made up my mind that no matter how much pain I was in I was going to see my friend. I got my mind and body together and I went to the hospital where James Hayley was. We went to the ICU. I had a boot on and I was on crutches. The pain I was in was indescribable. But I endured it, because I was coming to see my best friend—NO MATTER WHAT.

When I got to his room, his wife was there asleep in a chair. I knew she was exhausted, because she was asleep. She never would have slept otherwise. She would have stayed awake, no matter how she felt. But her body needed that little sleep. She had literally punished her body caring for her husband.

So, I see my friend, and he saw me, too. I just started crying. I couldn't help it. Here was my best friend who had been big and strong as a bull; now his body was frail and weak. The scene in his hospital room was depressing. His mother, along with other family members was there. His dear mom, a very strong, black woman was trying to be strong for everyone. But I could tell she was weak.

James recognized me, I know he did. But I couldn't say anything. All I could do was turn away from him crying. My tears was fallin' like a rain storm. Even though James' organs had begun shutting down some hours ago, he refused to give up the fight. He fought all the way to the end. I saw his valiant fight, but I just couldn't take it. I left and went home. I just couldn't take it anymore. James passed away that same night. We had his funeral soon afterward. Once again, my world had been crushed.

JAMES HAYLEY –

THE BEST FRIEND IN THE WORLD

Even as I write this book, and I think of my friend, James, my heart aches. He is no longer with us, but he will never be far from me—ever. He was just a true friend. We have known each other since we were boys. He was just about two years older than I was when we met. He was more like an older brother to me, than just a friend.

James represented power because he was a big dude and he protected me and other of his friends. He was real. He was very real. And even though he may not have gone in the right direction all of the time, he encouraged me and other friends of ours to pursue our dreams. He was there for me. I miss you Bro'.

By the time all of this happened, we had already moved away from Wayburn and Gray Streets, living in different places on our own. The one thing that remained was that we were still working on our goal to be successful with our music.

It was extremely hard after James passed away. I would sit around thinking to myself, "Was all this grinding, tears, and pain worth it?" I was so devastated that my phone would ring and ring all month and I didn't answer it. No matter how many times it rang I wouldn't answer it. But then one day when it rang, I finally answered it. The call was from my nephew Tone-tone. He asked, "Unc, how you holding up?"

I said, "Nephew, this is all fucked up! What now family? My mind is all screwed up again Nephew."

After a moment he said, "Listen Unc. Rich Gang, and the Bank Roll Mafia feelin' the movement. We on!"

I asked, "Drake and T.I.?"

"Yes," he said.

"Word?"

"Yeah, it's grind time. We are workin'. As soon as you get that boot and crutches off, get to work. DBF is working!"

And indeed, it was true. The album was called Tone-tone 11627 Wayburn and it was hosted by

DJ Drama. That was our address, where we lived—where all that music started. So, now if you check the MTV Jams videos you'll find our video entitled Tone-tone I Don't Know … Greatness Once Again.

It was at that moment right there that I knew our family needed to have its own legacy, a trend. We had promised Grandma Hattie that we would stick together and we committed ourselves to our music.

Our family has endured so much pain and even though I felt like quitting, I didn't. It would have been wrong to just stop and walk away leaving our family to endure through hard times and grief without me there to suffer and ache with them. It's not unusual for families to endure pain. Often when hard times come, families split up and go their separate ways and they hurt in secret and all alone, with no one to support or encourage them. And even though I, too, hurt and grieve, I promised my Grandma Hattie that we would stick together. My Uncle James died and his last words were to keep the family together. James Hayley, my best friend was there to support me and my nephews in our musical ventures. He passed away; but I believe that if he were still here, he would still be supporting us.

So I owe it to my Grandma Hattie, my Uncle James, and my friend James Hayley to stick with our family and make sure that others know of my family's well-deserved legacy.

Author's Note:

I felt like it was my duty to tell our family's story. The story of happiness, sadness, grief and pain; and how through it all we have emerged successful and honoring the ones who loved us and taught us and made us promise to stick together. I wanted the public to know just a little of our story and I did just that in writing this book. We have to recognize the truth.

To all my family and friends who are no longer with us, Rest In Peace. You may be gone but you will never be forgotten. "Grandma, we

have kept our promise we made to you before
you went to Heaven, to stick together."

'Low'

As this book is about some of the events that took place in my family, it is only fitting that some of them briefly share in this work. So in the pages below a couple of my family has penned words from their hearts.

GRAY STREET BOYS

By the time a young boy reaches the age of 13 years old, he could already have become a veteran in the street life. Everyone around him may already have wicked ways that can plague the very atmosphere.

Seeing this it made my decision easier and simple; mainly because my foundation was in place and I wasn't even aware of it. This was very tough – Ride, running through abandoned homes; riding scooters.

Be a reflection of what you'd like to receive. If you want love, give love. If you want truth, be truthful. Whatever you give out will always return to you.

****

Stay away from 'Still People'.

Still broke

Still complaining about the same situation

Still hating

Still running after the same man/woman

Still insecure

Still childish

Still lying

Still cheating

Still stuck on stupid

Still ain't going to change

Still and always will be a headache.

WHAT'S THE WORD?

****

I'm often mistaken a being mean, when I am friendly. I'm mistaken for being sad, when I want to be alone. I'm mistaken for being shy, when I'm quiet. Quit assuming and get to know me. In the words of the Temptations "I've Got Nothing But Love".

My Cloud Dweller, He has seen something good in a wretch like me; therefore, He's the greatest. Have a blessed life, my 'metropolitans'. Whoever makes it to my Savior's house put a prayer in for me. Thanks for all the love and blessings tossed my way.

In the words of Tupac, "Ya'll are Appreciated". Stay clean; clean from helmet to hooves; even the mittens.

Marcus Garner, one of 313 Rd's representatives—Have a blessed day my metropolitans and beyond.

~ Marcus Garner

****

What a great journey this has been. The Henderson Legacy is intact. From growing up in the 70s on Gray Street and experiencing a lot fun times, with other families like the Johnsons, Gardners, Purdues, Guins, Costners, and Thomas'.

Then came the 80s where our block was starting to change. People were moving out and the drugs were moving in. I became friends with the Rush family and the Walker family. I started boxing with the Johnson and King families; and with guys like Monte Beau, Coco, Ron Rush, Tyrone, Little Mack Perkins, Scubby Weestraw, Bow Legs Snoop, Lump Ron Moon, and our Coach, Blue Lewis, who fought Muhammad Ali; and the Goins Brothers, Mark and D'Earl.

Then came the 90s and we were moving. That's when the tragedy hit us. April 7th 1990.

~ Michael Mikeski Henderson

About the Author

Lawrence Gordon is a young man who is very active in the community and is committed to giving back to his community and helping wherever he can.

An intense author, Lawrence is real and unvarnished as he wields his pen to let his readers see life in its true light. He is a kind man who loves his children and family members very much.

When reading his story, you will see that he is raw, but only because he is passionate about his topic and unafraid to speak the truth about himself and others. Look for more from Lawrence Gordon, who has only begun to reveal his heart through the stories he writes.

Lawrence is also a member of The Umbrella Organization; a civic and community centered group. The Umbrella is a group of positive young men with multiple goals and they are committed to bettering themselves, their community, their loved ones, and those who are far and wide. They tap into everything from street knowledge, book knowledge, spiritual knowledge and political facets, as well.

"We are not a record label, nor are we a gang. Just a bunch of hustlin' ass young black men that came together as one. We are the Umbrella.

Follow Lawrence on Google+
Follow His Blog-
ww.lawrencegwordpress.wordpress.com

OUR BOND

Our family has a lot to be thankful for.

The memories through the years

The many times we've shared joy, laughter…

And many times sorrow and tears.

Grandma Hattie was the Rock of our family ties

A bond and memory so underrated

She bared her soul and honor so that we all could
be created

Uncle James and Grandma one day had a long
conversation

Then weeks after that we had our own family
congregation

As I look at the videos and photos of how we
used to be

I realize we split into groups, and now that's
what I see

Now it's our time to build what we once knew
was strong

Forgive one another and forget about

who was right and who was wrong.

Our bond was built on fairness, righteousness,

and also love

The two who built it for us, are now looking from

Heaven above

We all know they would want us to go back to

how we started

And to no longer be divided; no longer to be

parted

Someone has to do it; stand up and do what's

right

Where there's no winners or losers, just a bond

that's oh so tight

We don't choose our families; they are God's gift

to you

You just have to try to stay bonded and not let
the devil through
But if he does get through you have to push him
back out
And show him that forgiveness is what it's all
about
Once we come together, then it can all come back
Where there's God and love we're winners and
that is just a fact

Written by
LaTonja Gordon

DENBY HIGH SCHOOL

Top: Antonio, Mike J, Sean, Low Kib

Bottom: Denby Basketball Team with Coach Rubinstein Washington

Kevin Buddy

Daughter's Mom Denke Gaskins

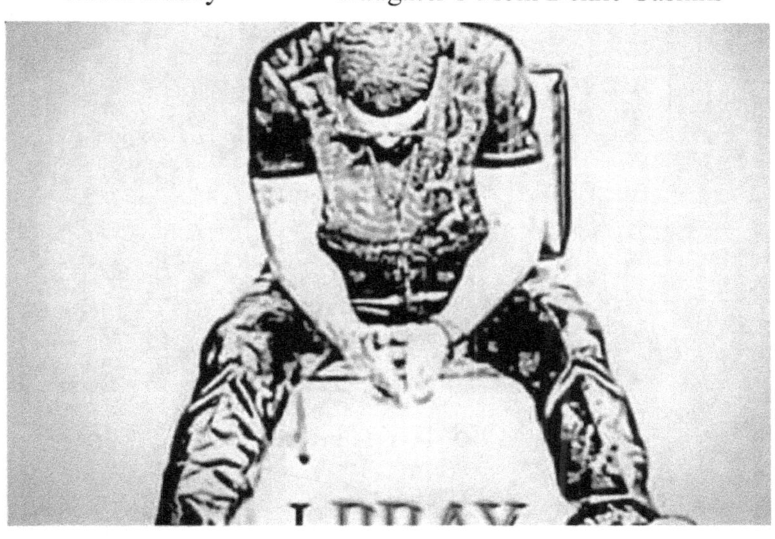

Gray Street

Old Town House

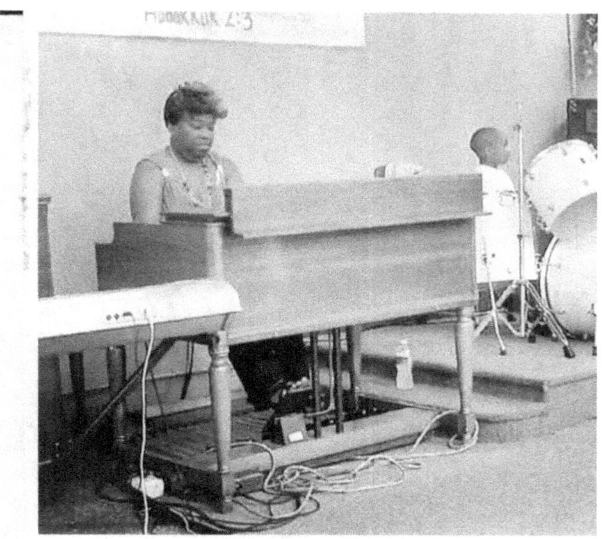

Mother Bobbie Gordon

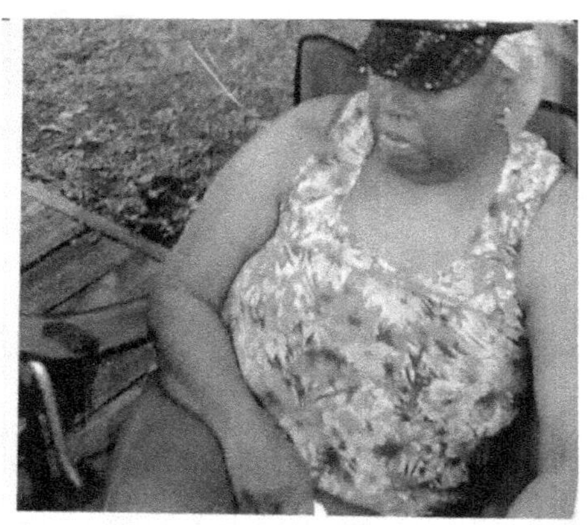

Mother Bobbie Gordon

Mom and Friend Mrs. Flo

Mom's Sis Auntie Louise

Mom's Sis Auntie Carleine Downs

MTV Jams Tone Tone Video

Lil Tony

My daughter Tanika Gordon

Antonio "Keith" Henderson

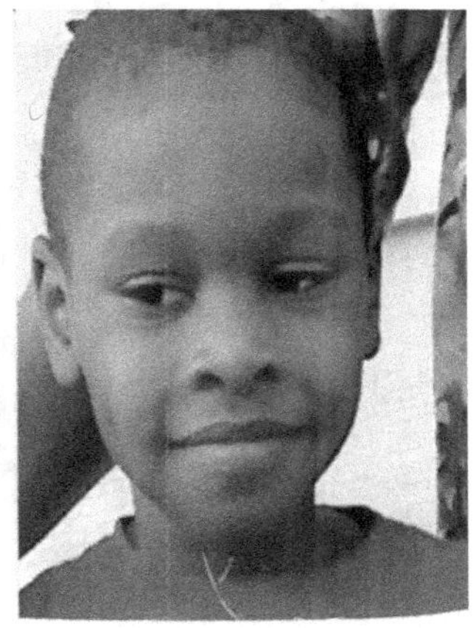

Amir Phelps

Wayburn House

Tone-Tone and TI

Tone-Tone

Sons Lawrence Jr. & Jaylenn Gordon

Grandmom Hattie Henderson

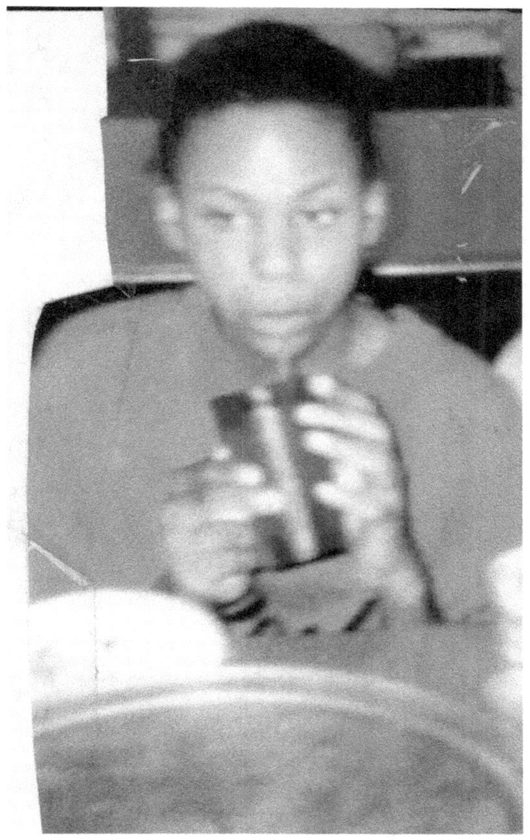

Lil Sister Danyell Gordon

Uncle James Henderson

Uncle James Henderson

WHAT'S THE WORD?

Uncle James Henderson

Sister Robin Gordon

Sister Latonja Gordon

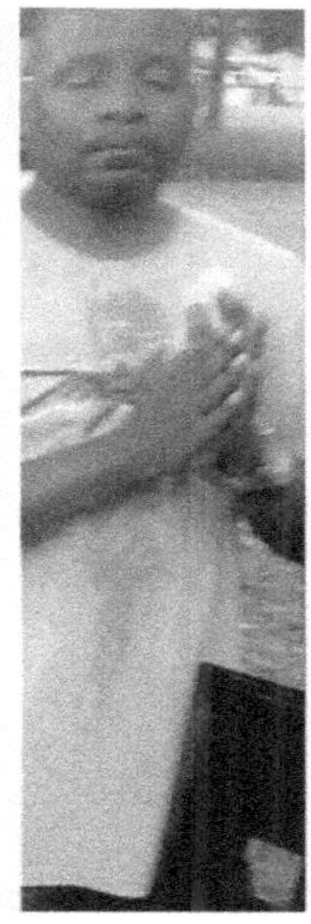

Older Brother D.K Henderson   Middle Bro Michael Henderson

Sis Latonja Gorson   Sis Deborah Henderson

Older Sis Carla Thomas Henderson

The Fort Studio

The Umbrella Organization

DBF Group

DBF

Family

Little Lawrence Gordon

Lawrence Gordon Barber

Best Friend James Hayley

James Hayley's Brother John Hayley

The Church I grew up in.

Family Church

Ferris State University

Cousin Maurice Downs   Lawrence Gordon

Cousin Tammy Sams

Friend of the family Dorothy "Dot" Rush

Cousin Osbin Jefferson